The Sleeping Bread

Story by Stefan Czernecki and Timothy Rhodes

Illustrated by Stefan Czernecki

Hyperion Books for Children

FIRST U.S. EDITION

10 9 8 7 6 5 4 3 2 1

ISBN: 1-56282-183-0 (trade)
ISBN: 1-56282-207-1 (lib. bdg.)

Library of Congress Catalogue Number: 91-75422

Book design by A. O. Osen
The artwork for each illustration is prepared in gouache art medium.
This book is set in 16-point Palatino type.

Once upon a time, in the sleepy little village of San Pedro, a bakery shop opened onto the square. It was called *Panadería el Milagro*, which means "Miracle Bakery," and a miracle did happen there. This is the story.

The busy shop was owned by a baker named Beto. He was a small, round man and he looked very much like the golden brown bread he baked every day.

Beto was busy from dawn to dusk, but he never complained. Many customers crowded into his shop to buy the fresh bread he made. He greeted each one cheerfully and always asked about the family.

In the evening, before climbing upstairs to sleep, Beto prepared for the following day. He made a great flat slab of dough, placed it into an enormous pan, covered it with a clean white cloth, and carefully placed it in the farthest corner of the dark bakery where it was warm and quiet.

Long before the rooster made his noisy greeting to the sunrise, Beto had returned to the bakery. Every morning he found that the flat dough had been transformed into a huge smooth pillowy loaf, and every morning he shoved the great loaf into the oven to bake.

As the bread baked, its sweet aroma wafted through the little town, and every morning the villagers awoke to the wonderful smell of fresh bread.

Soon the bakery was filled with jostling people and by mid-morning all the bread was gone except for two crusts. Beto saved these for Zafiro, a ragged beggar. The townspeople thought Zafiro was a nuisance, but Beto had a good heart and he was kind to him.

Every day, just before noon, Zafiro knocked timidly at the back door of the bakery, and every day Beto invited him in, gave him the bread, and sat down with him to listen to the old man's tales of his travels to faraway places and the wonders he had seen. No one knew where Zafiro had come from, but his shining blue eyes set him apart from the villagers of San Pedro.

As the time approached to celebrate the town's patron saint, many visitors arrived to enjoy the festival. The townspeople rounded up the beggars to keep them away from the visitors. Zafiro, however, continued to wander about, and his untidy appearance and his begging annoyed the strangers. "Who is this scruffy fellow?" they asked.

The townspeople were embarrassed and they called a meeting to decide what to do.

"He'll spoil the festival," said one, "and frighten away the visitors."

"We won't sell our wares," said another.

"Why does he stay in our village? He's not one of us," said the third.

In the end they asked Zafiro to leave.

Zafiro felt hurt and disappointed. "I shall move to the country," he thought. "I am better off by myself than with these people who are so unkind to me."

That afternoon Zafiro stopped at the bakery to say goodbye to Beto.

"My friend," the old man said sadly, "I fear I shall never return." As he told Beto the story about the villagers a single bitter tear fell into the water jar that Beto used for his baking.

That evening Beto prepared the dough as usual, but when he returned to the bakery in the morning and uncovered the pan, the bread had not risen. It was still flat and heavy. "What's wrong?" Beto thought.

He checked the flour to see if it had weevils. He checked the yeast. He poked the dough. "Why don't you rise?" he said.

He moved the pan closer to the warmth of the oven. It didn't help. The bread was still sleeping. There were no fresh bakery smells to greet the villagers that morning.

As the villagers awoke and crowded into the bakery they were angry and noisy. "Why is there no fresh bread?" they demanded.

They gathered around the bread pan and poked at the dough. "We must find a way to wake the sleeping bread," they muttered.

For three nights Beto watched over the bread pan, but each morning the bread still slept. The people grew worried. How could they celebrate the festival with no bread?

From high on the hill outside San Pedro, Zafiro watched as the people tried to wake the sleeping bread. First the village band marched up to the bakery and played as loudly as it could. The bread still slept.

Then the mayor walked up to the bakery and delivered a rousing speech in his great booming voice. The bread lay flat and silent.

The doctor clattered up to the bakery on his squeaky bicycle. He probed and prodded and kneaded and knotted the bread, but it slept on.

The priest came next and rattled through prayer after prayer, but the bread did not respond.

The village policeman rode up to the bakery on his lanky horse and ordered the bread to rise. He threatened to arrest the bread, but even that made no difference.

The blacksmith, the silversmith, the weaver, the sandal maker, the candle maker, each tried to wake the bread. Even a very old donkey braying loudly in the street had no effect. Finally everyone gave up and went home.

"Does anyone understand this mystery?" Beto asked himself that evening. He decided to seek the advice of San Simón the Miracle Maker. Quickly Beto packed a bag with some gifts that he was sure the saint would appreciate. Then he set out along a narrow path leading out of the village.

When Beto reached the shrine of San Simón he placed his gifts on the altar, lit the candles and the incense, and began to explain the problem of the sleeping bread. He talked so long and so monotonously that he finally put himself to sleep. In his dream San Simón came to him and told him that if he wanted an answer to his problem he must find Zafiro and ask him to return to the village. Beto woke with a start and rushed back to San Pedro.

Beto ran from house to house. "San Simón has spoken to me and I believe Zafiro can solve the mystery. We must get him back."

"What!" said the villagers. They could not understand how an old beggar could be of any use to them. "We do not want him back," they said.

However, Beto was persuasive and reluctantly the villagers agreed to look for him and ask him to return.

Early the next morning the villagers began their search. They looked everywhere without success. Night was not far away when Beto remembered that Zafiro had often talked of a secret place under a great old tree at the top of the hill.

Later that night he almost tripped over Zafiro who was sleeping with his back against the tree trunk. Zafiro had been watching the village and he knew about the bread.

"I'm not sure that I can help you," he said, "but because you were always kind to me I will go with you back to the village."

The two friends sat in Beto's shop and stared at the flat slab of dough. They could do nothing. Beto was so tired and disappointed that the tears began to roll down his cheeks. Watching his friend, Zafiro repeated an old saying that his mother had often told him.

"Whenever a tear be bitter, not sweet,
It should always be washed away."

Suddenly Zafiro stood up. "Tears! Tears are the answer," he shouted. "My bitter tear fell into the water jar," he exclaimed. "That is why your bread will not rise."

The two friends emptied and refilled the water jar, made the bread, covered it with a clean white cloth, and set it to rise. They intended to watch it all night but soon fell asleep. In the morning when Beto half opened his eyes he saw that the cloth had fallen to the floor. The bread was awake!

Beto built a fire and pushed the bread into the oven. Soon the aroma of baking bread brought all the villagers to the bakery.

"Zafiro has done this for us," Beto said.

"Ah," the crowd murmured, and they were grateful to the old man. "Stay! Stay!" they urged.

It was the day of the festival and the village square was crowded with townspeople and visitors, each eager to get the first glimpse of the colorful parade. When the costumed revelers came into view everyone exclaimed about the lavish dresses, the music, and the dancing. They were most in awe, however, of the patron saint who was being carried on a litter along the parade route. His costume was so dazzling and his manner so gracious that they wondered who he could be.

"This is truly a great man," the visitors muttered.

"You are fortunate to have such a person in your village," said one visitor.

"Yes," the villagers agreed.

The man behind the mask smiled and his blue eyes shone.